Highway

78

A. R. Fisher

CHAPTER 1

We've had these plans for over six months, and now the day is finally here. I haven't seen my friend Cathy in years, so the boys take it upon themselves to call her up and make plans. This is her vacation week off from work. I cannot wait to give her a giant hug and catch up on a lot.

Unlike me, Cathy had a job ready for her as soon as she graduated college. Not only did her scholarships pay for most of her education, but now she's making a buck in a half at the County Veterinarian Hospital. I am very proud of her, but am kind of jealous too. She makes life look so easy.

✦ ✦ ✦

Justin had offered to drive his SUV, even though I told him his gas mileage sucks. Bryan's car would have been better for the trees, but Justin's had the leg room, and floor space we needed.

"Is that everything?" Justin asked with his head still in the car.

"A few more," Bryan said handing him a medium size bag.

"Jeez, we are only going for four days. How much do we need?"

"It's this chick," Bryan said pointing at me.

"What? I want to be prepared."

"For a nuclear war?" Justin joked.

"Ha, ha, shut up and put the bags in the car," I said giving him two more, smaller bags.

"Your car better not die on us," Bryan stated as Justin closed the back hatch. "It's pushing a hundred and seventy thousand miles."

"It won't die. She's running like a stallion," he said touching the car.

"Let's hope so," I said to myself.

* * *

We were sitting on the couch not doing anything. The TV wasn't even on.

"Now what?" Bryan asked.

"We chill," I said.

"Can we do something? We have six hours."

"Like what?" Justin chimed in.

"Beach?" I suggested.

"Ehhhh," Bryan whined.

"Board game?" I tried.

"Fine, which one?" Justin said settling for the idea.

"Our version of Bridges. Like with an actual bridge in the game," Bryan said getting up.

We got out the board that Bryan made himself out of glue, tape, and cardboard. I am surprised the board has lasted these three years. Justin went downstairs to get his Matchbox cars.

"I'm Speedy," I yelled as soon as Justin walked through the door.

"Of course you are, aren't you always," Bryan said with a tone as if saying 'duh'.

"Yeah, just wanted to make it known."

Bryan gave me Speedy, and I put him on the start line. The boys got their cars and we were ready to go.

"Remind me again how to play?" Justin asked.

I found the notebook paper we used to write all the rules down. "The object is to get to the chest in the center. Must obey what the spaces ask or tell you. Don't get stuck on the bridge."

"That's it?" Bryan asked.

"Umm," I said turning the paper over. "Yeah, that's it."

"Those rules suck," Justin stated toward Bryan in a louder tone than expected.

"If I do remember correctly, you're the one who came up with the rules. I just wrote them down. Jerk," Bryan said in his defense.

I chuckled.

"Oh, what are you laughing at?" Justin said shooting me a dirty look.

"What? That was funny."

"Let's just make new rules then." Bryan's voice was back to normal

"I'd like to see you two work together," I said getting up.

I stood by the door already knowing that the game is never going to happen. Not with these two trying to work together. I stayed by the door listening to the boys trying to come up with new rules. Bryan would suggest a rule then Justin would pretty much bash it into the ground. It was amusing for a little while, until they completely got off the topic of the game and somehow got into the subject of who's wrestler on WWE was better. I went into the living room thinking it would be a little quieter. Nope. Actually, it's gotten louder. I turned the TV on and jacked the volume up to drown out their obnoxious boy behavior.

Justin is my brother's closest friend. When Andrew told me he signed up for the Army I was proud, but scared. Andrew gave Justin strict orders to be my guardian at all costs. If I could be with Justin I would, but because we have that brother/sister relationship, it would be too weird.

Bryan is Justin's younger brother. He came into the picture about a year after Justin. He's two years older than me, and because him and I aren't so close I would be okay with him asking me out, if he ever wanted to.

The arguing continued for a good forty–five minutes. I couldn't even drown them out anymore. I muted the TV and ran into the den. I quickly folded the cardboard up and put it in its box.

"Game over. I never want to hear of this game ever again," I yelled, but I shut them up.

"You're the one who suggested we play it."

"I will not make that mistake again."

* * *

We were all on the couch. I was in the middle leaning closer to Bryan. After a while I put my head on his shoulder.

"What time is it?" I asked.

"Four," Bryan said.

"Want to go for an early dinner then we can be on our way," I said.

"Okay with me," Justin said looking to Bryan.

"Only if I can sit in the back with Heather."

"Get your butts up. Let's go. And no, you will sit up front with me."

Chapter 2

I had my normal chicken fingers and fries. Bryan got a burger. Typical boy food, and Justin got shrimp. He let me mooch off of him if I shared too. Justin paid for both of us on the way out the door. With full tummies and our legs stretched we got back out to the car and prepared ourselves for an hour ride at least.

We left the restaurant around six, which is what we wanted. I was able to get Justin to allow Bryan to sit in the back with me. It would have been a lonely ride if he sat up front with his brother. We played the ABC game once we got on the highway. We would yell out random words on street signs that started with whatever letter we were on. The only exceptions were letters q, u, x, y, and z. These were the only letters that could be contained with in the word.

"What letter are we on?" I asked.

"Q," Justin said.

We stopped at a red light and I scanned all the signs that were stuck in the ground around the stoplight's pole.

"Barbeque!" I yelled.

"Where?" Bryan said looking around excited.

"No, for the letter Q."

"Oh, ha."

We got through the alphabet then Bryan started with Eye Spy.

"You can't spy on anything outside the car," I said.

"Why not?" Bryan pouted.

"Ummm, because it goes by too fast. I won't have time to spy it."

"Duh," Justin added.

Bryan leaned forward and punched Justin in the arm. "Smartass."

"Couldn't help it. You're lucky I'm driving or you would be hurting right now."

"Oooo, a threat?" Bryan said raising his hands up in surrender.

"Shut up, both of you."

I turned to the window and saw the sky become a light navy color. "What time is it?"

"We should have left later. We are right in the middle of rush hour traffic, and it's eight o'clock. Wait . . ."

"It's after rush hour?"

"It's been two hours and we aren't even half way," Bryan whined.

"Dude, relax," I said, "we have bigger problems right now."

I leaned toward the front and looked out the front window to get a better view of the traffic.

"We'll get there by midnight at the earliest," Bryan said with a hint of sarcasm.

There was nothing but break lights in front of us, and an endless line of headlights behind us. The jerk off right behind us didn't know he had his high beams on.

"Dude," Justin said flipping his mirror. "There is a blue light on your dashboard that indicates your high beams are on. That would drive me nuts."

I giggled. I like the way Justin got frustrated sometimes. He shot me the evil eye in the mirror, but I still smiled.

"Take the next exit," Bryan said.

"I'm in the left lane. Getting over to an exit is going to suck, a lot."

"Why is this piece of crap in the fast lane anyway?"

"Say one more negative thing about my car and I will come back there."

A second threat from Justin was always put into action. Bryan and I knew our limits.

There was one time last year Justin had locked Bryan in a closet at home. Bryan deserved it, but when we opened the door the bleach bottle had fallen over. Justin had pushed him in there, for a time out. That was Bryan's favorite spot in the house, or it seemed like it. Every time I came home from school Justin was leaning against the hall closet. Bryan was sitting in the big yellow mop bucket janitors usually use, the few mops and brooms had fallen over from the slamming of the door pinning Bryan from moving anywhere. He was lucky the bottle was almost empty or his hair would have turned 'bleach' blonde.

"Justin?"

"Yeah Heather."

"Where are your parents? You and Bryan never talk about them."

The car became a dead silence that was being broken only by the sound of honking horns. I look at Justin in the mirror then turned to Bryan.

Chapter 3

"We don't remember our parents. Not our biological parents. Bryan and I were adopted."

"Oh?"

The car became silent again. "So it's been just you two?"

"We've had families come and go," Bryan said.

"Once I became of working age I told Bryan that we couldn't spend a dime. Me working was our way home."

The traffic was still moving, slowly, but moving.

"How did you and Andrew meet?"

"We were working at a Honda detail place. He's told you about that. We were partnered up for most of the jobs, and worked really well together. Friendship, and brotherhood followed."

"I miss him," I said. "It's only been two months. This deployment will last forever."

"You'll get through it. When we get back we should send him a card from all of us. We can take a silly picture and put it inside for him."

I started to tear up with tears of fear for Andrew and happiness because of what Justin has done for me so far.

"Thank you," I said without thinking.

"For what?" he asked.

"Everything."

I felt Bryan's arm around my shoulders. He held me close as my stress that has been locked up, finally came out. I was having a breakdown. The tears were rolling and the sobbing turned to all out crying. I could hear Justin turn the music down and his voice fill the car. Bryan's arm was strong, yet gentle as he held me, filling me with a certain security that I haven't had since Andrew left.

"I'm sorry," I said catching my breath as the car rolled forward.

"Don't be. Everyone needs a breakdown. Yours is just under different circumstances," Justin said.

The car crept forward behind the eighteen-wheeler in front of us, in the fast lane.

"Why is this guy in the fast lane?"

"Does it matter," Bryan said. "We aren't going anywhere."

"Heather, can you call Cathy. Tell her we might be a little late."

"Tell her we will be there tomorrow," Bryan said. I hoped he was joking.

"You're being a Smartass again," Justin said looking in the rear view mirror.

"Dude, you really think we will get there in three hours. With the rate this traffic is moving, we'll be lucky to get there by midnight."

"That's it," Justin said hitting the steering wheel. He hurled himself backwards over the center console. I didn't really know what was happening until Justin opened the door.

"Justin, relax," Bryan said.

"Justin," I squeaked while quickly following them out of the car. The car jerked on its suspension and knocked me back into my seat. It jerked again. "Justin, stop!"

I got out of the car and stood to the side of them. There was a terror in Bryan's eyes I have never seen before. I have never seen this side of Justin either.

"Stop!" I yelled.

They both looked at me. Justin's hands were still attached to Bryan's shirt.

"Let go," I said softly, but sternly placing my hand on his. "What's wrong?"

"I'm sick of this kid being a smart ass all the time."

"It's part of my personality dude, chill," Bryan said. Both his hands were up in surrender.

"Let him go," I said sternly, word for word. "It doesn't look like we are going anywhere soon. Turn the car off and we'll sit out here," I suggested trying to calm the mood.

Justin roughly let his brother go and lightly pushed him back into the car.

"I said we. All of us," I clarified.

"I can't look at him right now." Justin closed the car door and sat against his front tire. I starred into the tinted window seeing my reflection, not Bryan.

Chapter 4

The guy next to us in the next lane allowed me to lean against his car's tire. I thanked him and sat across from Justin. My knees were bent, my back against the tire and my arms rested against my knees. I lay my head back and kept my eyes on Justin. He hasn't made eye contact with me since I sat down.

"Justin."

"What," he said through gritted teeth.

"I think Bryan has been in 'time out' long enough. I'm letting him out."

The door to the car opened before I got up.

"You're done in time out," I said with a smile.

"Good, it was getting a little stuffy in there."

"Stop," I said nodding towards Justin with a straight face. I looked over at Justin waiting for a reaction like before. Nothing. "What happened before?"

"Nothing," Justin said.

"I wasn't talking to you. What did you do?" I asked Bryan.

"I didn't do anything."

"Liar," Justin said through gritted teeth.

"You," I pointed to Justin. "Shut up."

"I don't know what I did. Honest."

"I am not going to be the siblings' counselor tonight. Do both of you understand?"

"Yeah," Bryan said.

"Yes," Justin pouted.

"Dude, what's your problem?" I asked holding my hands out.

"Nothing," Justin grunted.

"You're not going anywhere, anytime soon. If you have something to get off your chest, mine as well do it. You have never acted that way towards Bryan before. What's the problem?"

"The monster isn't coming back. Is it?" Bryan asked.

I was going to ask, but stopped myself mid breath. *Let them work this out.*

"No it's not," Justin growled.

"It is," Bryan said.

"Shut up," Justin said.

Bryan turned to the car and climbed back in, and slammed the door behind him. I looked to Justin who was starring at the car's tire next to us. I sat down next to him. "Justin?"

He looked at me.

"You don't have to hold back anymore. You and Bryan are old enough to be on your own."

"I'm not holding back anything," Justin said.

"What's the monster your brother asked about?"

I could tell this question caught him off guard. "None of your damn business."

"You've known me since I was little and you still can't talk to me."

"I will talk to you if it concerns you," he yelled.

"Does Andrew know about the monster?" I shot back.

"Why wouldn't he?"

"He wouldn't let you be my guardian if he didn't trust you. You've been able to control whatever monster you have, but don't you think it's safer for everyone if *we* all knew what *it* is?" I said trying to keep the mood calm. I heard the car door open and jumped at its sound.

"Relax," Bryan said slowly coming over to us. "Everything okay?"

"Fine," Justin said sternly. Bryan came over and sat down next to me.

"Talk to me," I pleaded putting my hand on Justin's shoulder.

"You will find out soon enough."

Justin got up and walked into the headlights. A lot of people had their cars turned off now. There were streetlights, but not where we were 'parked'.

"Justin," I squeaked and started walking after him.

"Let him cool off," Bryan said sweetly while he held my shoulders.

Chapter 5

The car was off with the keys in the ignition. I turned the key to click to turn the car on to see the clock. Its read midnight and Justin isn't back yet. It's been a half hour or so and I am really starting to get worried. Bryan doesn't seem to mind that his brother has been gone for this long.

"Should we go look for him?" I asked.

"He's fine. He used to do this every time we argued. There was a time he left for a week and came back."

"What about you? Who took care of you?"

"Because we didn't have a set family, Justin taught me everything really early on. I was eleven when he left for that week."

"Eleven?"

"Yeah, but I didn't mind the alone time," he smiled.

Bryan and I were in the car. He had got himself somewhat comfortable shoved between the back of the driver's seat and where I sat. I was leaning against the interior door of the car.

"Do you think Cathy is starting to worry?" I asked.

"Let me check." He fought with his jeans pocket to get him phone out. "No, she's not worried."

"How you know?"

"She texted me," he said showing me the screen of the phone.

"So, I guess you told her we are stuck in a non-moving traffic jam."

"Yeah, something like that."

He pulled himself out of the hole and sat on the seat at my feet.

"You tired?" he asked me.

"Ehhhh, you?"

"A little. Sitting in a car is so boring. At least when you're driving you have stuff going by to look at."

"Let's go see what the hold up is?" I suggested.

"Like up there," he pointed to the flashy lights.

"Yeah, what do ya say? You up for a little adventure?"

"Sure, let me just grab the keys. I'll text him too, just so he knows where we are."

We walked through the alleyway of cars on the dotted white line. I tried my best not to look in the car windows as we passed. There were some I couldn't resist and looked inside the car, trying to avoid any eye contact. The first car in front of the middle lane was a blue pickup truck with two thick white lines running down the roof onto the hood. I looked into the car and saw a scary man sitting in the driver's seat. He was wearing a dirty white tank top. I caught a glimpse of a flannel shirt on the passenger seat. Thank god his windows were up or he would have grabbed my shirt and threatened me for looking at him.

Bryan and I got to the caution tape that was tied onto those big orange road construction barrels. Looking beyond the tape is showing me why this traffic is so bad. I can't count the amount of vehicles with flashy lights. I can't even tell how many cars were involved. The cars were mangled balls of bent steel and broken bodies. I wanted to start looking for the cause of the accident, but this wasn't really any of my business.

"We've seen it and know why it's taking so long. Let's head back," Bryan said.

I think he said that just to get me back to the car for sleep. I didn't pass the blue pickup truck again. I went down pass a white Honda instead.

When our SUV came into view Justin was leaning against the passenger window.

"Hey, so what's going on up there?" he asked.

"Major carnage," Bryan said.

"Bad accident," I said in human language. "Hopefully we'll be moving by tomorrow."

"Mine as well rest up." Bryan suggested leading me to the car. He held his hand up and helped me in. I lie down on the seat and look to him and Justin.

"Aren't you coming?"

"Be right there," Bryan said as Justin slowly closed the door.

Even though I was comfortable, I really wanted my puppy that was in the bag behind the seat. With a few grunts I pulled my doggie from my bag and grabbed the blanket usually left behind in Justin's car.

The car door opened as soon as I was resettled.

"Comfortable enough?" Justin asked and climbed over the center console to the driver's seat.

"Warm enough?" Bryan added plopping down next to me.

"Yes and could do a little more warmth."

"Wipe that smile off your face Bryan," Justin said getting situated in the front seat.

"Oops," Bryan said low so only I could hear it. "You do know these seats fold flat."

"No?"

"Watch this."

Bryan looked to his right and pulled the seat lever up with the sound of a *click*. He leaned back, and pushed the seat back all the way with his hand. I opened the blanket and gave some to him.

"You're the one who is cold."

"You're the one with the body heat. Come here," I said holding up the side of the blanket. I think he was hesitating, waiting for approval from Justin. He wanted to look up to the rear view mirror, but didn't. Instead he lay next to me putting his arm under my head. I turned to my side facing away from him. I kind of wanted him to put his other arm over my waist, but Justin was watching.

"I'll see you tomorrow," Bryan whispered.

I smiled and pushed myself a little closer.

Chapter 6

I woke up to a brisk chill in the air. I was still lying on Bryan's arm. As comfortable as I was I slowly sat up not wanting to wake Bryan. The air touched my hands that had finally warmed up, and made them almost instantly cold again. I looked at Justin who had reclined the driver's seat as far back as it would go, and he was asleep too. I got my cell phone out that was resting in my shoe. I had no messages or missed calls from Cathy. I looked at the boys, took Bryan's sweatshirt and put it on over my thin long sleeve shirt, put my shoes back on and went towards the door. I put my phone in the pocket of Bryan's baggy sweatshirt and reached for the door handle. I put my hand on the handle and gently pulled hoping its noise wouldn't wake the boys. I felt the latch of the door open, without the normal loud click.

"Heather," I heard one of the boys say as I climbed out. Even though one of them was awake, I closed the door softly and headed towards the accident site.

The air was cold, quiet and still. I pulled the hood up and tied the strings to keep out the draft, putting my hands in the big pocket on the front of the sweatshirt to try to warm them up. I was coming up on the blue pickup truck with the scary man in it. I did everything in my will power to not look inside, but I did. There was no one in there. It was empty. *He was crazy enough to abandon his car. Maybe he walked home.*

"Turn around slowly, and no one will get hurt."

I felt something poking me in the back. Tears came to my eyes before I started turning around.

"I uh."

"Do you like my car?" he asked in a really creepy tone.

"The color is nice." My voice was shaky letting him know how scared I was.

"Do you want it?" he growled.

"No," I teared.

"You look at my car or me again I will not hesitant," he smirked waving his gun before lowering it. He took a step closer, raising his hand to the handle on the truck. I moved out of the way lowering my eyes and started back to the safety of Justin's SUV. I wiped away remaining tears as I walked hoping the boys wouldn't notice that I had been crying. My walk turned into a run without me noticing. The tears started again. I ran with my head low until I hit something. The hands grabbed my arms and wouldn't let go.

"Whoa, easy killer." It was Bryan.

"Are you okay?" Justin asked coming over.

"Sure," I said still shaking.

"Liar."

"I've always been bad at lying," I said trying for a smile.

"Are you okay?" he asked again.

"He threatened me."

"Who?" Bryan asked slowly letting go of my arms.

"There's a guy up there in a blue pick up truck. He didn't like me looking at it," I said faster than I should of.

"Really? What an asshole," Justin said.

"Next time, tell us where you are going," Bryan said sweetly. "I saw you leave."

"The cold woke me up."

"Heather, it's sixty degrees," Justin said.

"It was cold when I got up," I said submissively.

"It's two in the morning. Can we all attempt to go back to bed?" Bryan suggested opening the door for me.

"A little while," I said. "Still a little traumatized."

Bryan went inside leaving the car door cracked. I looked at Justin and he looked at me knowing something was off. He brought me in for a hug and I literally melted in his embrace.

"Sorry," I said.

"You have to understand that it's my job to protect you. I can't do that if I'm not there."

"I know."

He hugged me tighter and I felt him lean against the car. I finally wrapped my arms around him and my ear into his chest. I could hear the comforting sound of his heartbeat.

"Are we relaxed enough to sleep?"

"Yes, only if you sleep with me. Please?"

He loosened his hug and looked down at me. "If you want me to."

I took his hand and opened the car door. Bryan was leaning against the car's interior door looking at us. "Can we turn the radio on?"

"Sure, but not too long. This car has to start," Justin said.

"This thing better start," Bryan shot back.

"Justin, my phone is fully charged. Well just play music on it," I said calming the mood.

Justin shot Bryan a dirty look then sat down next to me. My head was leaning on Bryan's shoulder as I looked for iHeart radio. The music started playing and I put the phone on the Bryan's leg, knowing I've accomplished my mission.

I was staring at the window opposite of us until I felt Justin take hold of my hand. "Don't fight it."

I looked at him with tired eyes and shifted to get comfortable on his lap. He placed his hand on my shoulder and I closed my eyes.

"Thank you," I said finding his hand on my shoulder to hold.

Chapter 7

I woke to the car jerking on its suspension. My eyes shot open and looked at the window. My vision was still a little blurry with sleep, but I could make out a human form on the outside of the car.

"Justin," I said in a surprisingly calm tone.

"Stay here," he said getting up.

I felt an arm pull me in the opposite direction in which I was laying. Bryan held me close as I watched Justin leave the car. The first stranger that came to mind was the guy that held a gun to my back. I tensed up when I remembered the gun. I tried to sit up, but Bryan's arms wouldn't let me.

"Justin," I whispered. "Justin, wait," I said getting up.

I had caught Bryan off guard and was able to scoot off the seat closer to the door.

"No, Heather."

Bryan hugged me from behind. I could see out the window and felt the car jerk to one side as Scary man slammed Justin against the car.

"Bryan," I pleaded," You don't understand. That guy has a gun."

Before I finished the sentence, Bryan was out the door. I crawled to the farthest corner away from the door and held the blanket with my dog. I hugged my knees while tears wet my cheeks. The grunting noises outside became louder as did the voices. I slowly let go of my knees and extended myself up to see out the far windows. I saw people; strangers come to help Justin, and Bryan. I slowly crawled to the edge of the seat in awe of what was happening. I put my shoes on the floor and walked on my knees to the door. I pulled on the handle until the latch let go.

"Heather," Bryan yelled. He then pointed to the front tire. "Get him inside."

I knelt down. He was sitting, leaning against the wheel. His head dangled and his hair was wet with sweat.

"Justin."

I reached for his hand then saw his head try to lift. "Don't' try. Come on."

I pulled on his arm and he was able to get up, but he didn't stand up straight. He put his hand against the car and I stayed by his side to catch him if needed.

"Can you climb in?"

I got behind him and lifted a knee to the car's floor. I lightly pushed him in the rest of the way. I then saw there was no room for him to lie down.

"Do these seats fold into the floor?"

"Car is too old," he grunted.

He laid himself on the floor between the two seats and didn't move. I climbed in and closed the dor at the same time a gunshot went off, enhancing the slamming of the door. I looked through the window at the four or so guys on the Scary man. I didn't see Bryan. I quickly looked to Justin, whose swollen eyes were closed. I turned back to the door and outside to find Bryan.

"Bryan," I yelled as soon as I opened the door.

I cautiously made my way closer to the group of guys. The Scary man was pinned between the group of guys and a car. I don't know where the gun is, or Bryan.

"Bryan," I said as tears filled my eyes.

"Heather," I heard and my stomach flipped. I looked around, growing more nervous that I was hearing things. I finally found him leaning against a car close to the group trying to hold back Scary man. I ran to him and frantically looked him over.

"You're not hurt. Are you?"

"No, just beat up."

I heard a stampeded of footsteps come from the crash sight. There were seven or so cops that rushed in to break up the fight. Four cops stood between the mob and the Scary man while the other two put handcuffs on Scary man.

Once they dragged Scary man off, a policeman came over to Bryan and me. "You guys okay?"

"Yeah," Bryan said wincing as he leaned forward.

"Easy buddy," Policeman said. "May I look?"

He lifted Bryan's shirt and revealed a gnarly bruise starting to form on his ribs. "Looks like you may have a few bruised ribs son. We should get you to the hospital."

"I'm not going anywhere unless Justin and Heather come with me."

"Is Justin okay?" Policeman asked.

"He's in the car," I said pointing to Justin's SUV.

I went to help Bryan up when Policeman stopped me. "I'll get him. You lead the way."

Something about the way Policeman smiled gave me a sense of relief. The kind of relief that makes me and everyone else on this road feel safe.

Chapter 8

I opened the door and climbed inside. Justin hadn't moved since I left him.

"Justin," I whispered getting into the car. "Open your eyes."

I got on the seat above and next to him. Policeman and Bryan were still standing in the car's open door. I put my hand on Justin's and looked to Bryan. He started to slowly climb up with Policeman's help.

"Justin," Bryan said putting his hand on his brother's leg and shaking it a little. "Come on buddy."

"I'm sorry," Justin choked out.

"Justin," I said with tears in my eyes.

"Don't be," Bryan said. "You have to keep me in my place."

I looked to Bryan when he spoke and saw him holding his ribs. It made me think of Justin's possible injury. I slowly lifted Justin's shirt after moving his hand and saw a red bruise forming over his left ribcage. I could see an indent of where a rib used to be. *His is worse than Bryan's.*

"Officer O'Ryan, do you read me?"

I looked to the walkie-talkie on O'Ryan's shoulder.

"O'Ryan to base," he said pushing the button.

"The tow trucks have to do a round about around the traffic. They have told us about another two hours.

He looked at us. "Will you kids be okay?"

"Would you be able to get us to a hospital?"

"If the tow trucks can't get here. The ambulances may not be able to either. We'll have to get them a way through this traffic."

"He may not make the two hour wait," I teared looking to Justin.

"I'll call the ambulance. If we can't get this traffic moving they will have to walk to this car. I have to go back to my car to make the call. I will be right back."

O'Ryan held out his hand until I grabbed it. He gently squeezed my fingers until the tips turned red. I'll be right back."

He closed the door and I watched him walk away. I looked to Justin when O'Ryan was no longer in my sight. I was on my stomach on the seat above him and gently traced the back of his hand with my pointer finger. I was able to crack a smile when I looked to his peaceful face. It was peaceful, but was bruised, and broken too. Both his eyes looked swollen. His left eye was worse. His nose looked different than before. *I'm sure it's broken*, and his lip was cut and swelling a little. I looked back down to Justin's hand and noticed the bruises and cuts on his knuckles. *At least he was able to get a few punches in.*

"Oh Justin. Look at you," I got out as more tears started, making talking a little more difficult.

Bryan was sitting closest to the door trying to find a comfortable spot that wouldn't affect his rib.

"Just lay down. It won't put any pressure on it," I said.

"There isn't enough room on the other side of him and I can't get up on that seat," he said pointing to the seat we had laid flat for a bed.

"I'll help you."

Bryan got himself situated on the other side of me. It wasn't easy getting him up and I might have done more damage, but at least now he's comfortable. He put the arm on his uninjured side behind his head, and placed the other one on his upper thigh and looked at the ceiling. I watched him as he slowly fell asleep, not even realizing I was looking at him. Even though these two were in the car with me, I felt unbelievably alone, and vulnerable.

I was in deep thought, or slightly asleep when Justin quietly said my name. I jerked awake as if a loud noise had woken me, and became aware of where I was. I rolled away from Bryan to look down at Justin. "Help?"

"It's coming Justin."

I looked down at him and him barely up at me. His eyes were half open, but were empty. There was no sparkle. No life. I put the palm of my hand to his cheek and felt how warm he was. I could feel the body heat radiating off of him. I tried to relax myself enough to go to sleep, but only enough for a very light sleep. The softest of sounds would wake me every time I closed my eyes. I eventually gave up and opened my eyes. I sat up on my elbows and looked to Justin. Even though he is asleep I can still see the pain on his face and saw small beads of sweat forming on Justin's forehead. I guess with a broken rib or ribs the body reacts with a high fever. Or maybe this has gone from bad to worse. The only thing I could do for him was to make him comfortable, and pray.

* * *

I woke up not remembering or even knowing how I was able to get to sleep. I felt a hand on my cheek before opening my eyes. I was hoping it was Justin's, but didn't want to be disappointed if it was Bryan.

I lifted my head off the seat as I became more awake and could hear the boy's breathing fill the interior of the car. Bryan's was heavier than Justin's. I sat up and looked at Bryan and saw how fast his breathing really was. Faster than what it should be for sleep. I slid closer to Bryan and eased myself next to him so I didn't wake him or cause him anymore pain. I looked at Bryan from where I had laid on his uninjured arm and had a hunch that he was having a nightmare.

"Heather," I heard Justin say.

"I'm okay," I whispered

I heard Justin grunt softly.

"Don't try to move." I told him as I turned away from Bryan being careful not to hit his body to face Justin.

"I uh, I tried to wake you before, but you looked so peaceful."

"I was kind of awake when you did that. I haven't really slept tonight. Been too worried about you and Bryan."

"When is the ambulance coming?" he asked in a weak voice.

"O'Ryan said a few hours."

"Whose O'Ryan?" he asked looking tired.

"A policeman that helped Bryan and I."

"Is Bryan okay?" he asked trying to sit up.

"No, don't sit up. He's a little beat up, but better than you," I demanded putting my hand on his shoulder.

"It's really starting to hurt. I can't take a deep breath. It hurts with every small movement I try to make."

"Then don't make those movements," I smiled.

"Don't be a Smartass," he grunted, but I could still here that hint of sarcasm in his voice.

"O'Ryan went to call the ambulance."

"How, long ago, was that."

"Twenty minutes or so."

"This traffic needs to start moving," he said with more grunting, than talking. He put his hand to his ribs and sat up leaning against the car door for support.

"I told you not to move," I said louder then I intended.

I quickly turned to the bang on the door. It was O'Ryan. He was banging on the window with a worried look on his face. I crawled over, unlocked the door and pulled the handle.

"What's wrong? Is the ambulance coming?"

"Yes," he said monotone.

"Then, what's, the problem?" Justin asked slowly, grunting every word.

"That guy we hand cuffed . . ." he said then pausing.

"Yeah."

"He's gone."

Chapter 9

I sat back and felt the seat hit the back of my knees. When the seat caught me I scooted back until I felt Bryan's arm against my lower back.

"He tried to kill me." My voice was shaky. I brought my knees to my chest and felt the anxiety building up.

"Where did he go?" Bryan asked.

"Bryan," I said turning to him. "Bryan, you had a nightmare."

"Where is he?" Bryan asked through clenched teeth. I gave him the biggest hug I could, trying to avoid squeezing his midsection. I looked over to O'Ryan as I slowly helped Bryan sit up. He grunted, but wouldn't give up, until he was sitting upright.

"We don't know."

"There was no one in the car with him," Bryan shot back holding his ribs.

"It's not my job to make sure someone stays in the car."

"It is your job to keep him in custody, dammit."

Why hasn't Justin said anything?

I looked back to where he was leaning against the door of the car. He was passed out slumped over awkwardly on his injured rib. I made sure Bryan was okay sitting up by himself and went over to my Justin.

"Justin," I said trying to stay calm. I brushed his bangs away from his forehead to see his eyes. They were closed, but I could still see, feel his pain. "Justin," I said a little louder.

I heard Bryan slowly making his way over. My first thought was we had to move him, I just didn't know how we were going to do it. The space is so tight. I could hear Justin breathing become almost difficult. He began making small wheezing breaths still in a steady pattern.

"These seats fold down. Don't they?" Bryan asked looking towards the bed seat in a frantic voice.

"Justin said they didn't. I don't know how we are going to lay him down without doing any further damage."

"I want to try. They have to fold down or come out or something."

Bryan slid to the end of the seat/bed and held his left rib. He cringed when he got his knees on the floor. So did I.

"Take it easy. Justin isn't the only one who's banged up mister."

"Sorry mom."

Bryan had to bend over to look at the lever next to the seat

"Why don't you tell me what you're trying to do? Let me do the lifting and what not," I suggested.

"No, you stay there. Try to hold Justin in a way to get him off that injured rib."

"And you?" I yelled.

"Let me do it," O'Ryan said.

We all looked at him. "I used to have a car like this. I know how the seats come out. May I?"

"By all means."

We did some rearranging of bodies so O'Ryan could get in. I stayed where I was hoping to stay out of the way. I was able to straddle Justin to use my body to hold him against the interior wall of the car. When I heard a small click, I felt my stomach flip and saw a seat come out of place. I looked to Bryan and smiled. O'Ryan gently placed the three person seat in the back with our clothes bags. Bryan slowly came over to me as I started to get myself off Justin. Bryan held his brother's shoulders as moved off him. I was about to pull Justin's ankles when O'Ryan came over and offered. I'm glad he did because Justin would have been too heavy for me to drag his dead weight, even just a few inches.

"Thank you."

"Ready, on three." O'Ryan gripped Justin's ankles under his jean covered legs. "One, two," on three O'Ryan gently pulled Justin's ankles toward him until Justin was lying flat on the floor. Justin grunted until he was still again.

"Justin, I'm sorry."

His left hand grabbed his right ribs as he curled to that side.

"No," I grabbed his arm. "Lay flat."

Once Justin was back to sleep I felt relief when his breathing was steady and quiet. I felt O'Ryan's arm around my shoulder and looked to him. He smiled and slowly started making his way to the exit.

"Wait, don't go."

"You guys need the room. I'll stand out here until help arrives."

"How do we protect ourselves?" I asked.

Now that Justin was breathing normal I could think of our safety.

"Me," O'Ryan said. "I will not leave this car's side until the traffic moves, or this guy is caught, or dead."

"We have to get through this night though."

"It's four am now. I heard them say everything should be clear before rush hour traffic."

"You said the ambulance would be here before then," I confirmed.

"It should be," he said.

"It better be," I heard Bryan say under his breath.

I turned and saw a pillow from where I was sitting. I lay down to reach it. I sat back up and placed it under Justin's head. I went to pick his head up and could hear the quiet wheezing breaths again.

"There's got to be an easier way to help him breath?"

"Turn him to his uninjured side," O'Ryan suggested.

I did as O'Ryan suggested, with little help from Bryan and saw the dip Justin's injured rib made through his shirt.

"Let's put a pillow under him so his body is straight, or two pillows," I said tapping the floor and sliding my hand towards Justin's ribs.

After Justin was situated I made sure to position his arms in a way that could hold me then lay next to him, folding his arms around me.

"Heather," Justin said low and groggy.

"I'm here," I said squeezing his arms around me.

"Ambulance?" he got out.

"They are coming," Bryan said. He was leaning against the back of the passenger seat. The driver's seat was reclined back from when Justin slept before he got hurt. He held his ribs as he sat up with the help of his one arm and pulled himself over to me. He slowly laid down putting his arm over me but rested his hand on Justin's shoulder. "They are coming buddy."

The three of us lay quiet. I was dozing off when I heard a faint siren coming from the direction of the never-ending traffic.

"You hear that?" I asked Bryan.

"I sure did," he said. "They are coming buddy."

"I know," he said low. "I, can hear, them."

He was still talking in broken sentences, but at least he was talking. I looked at O'Ryan who had just started closing the door.

"Wait," I said. "You said you weren't going to leave until that guy is caught."

"I'm not leaving. I am moving to the front seat."

He closed the door. I sat up so I could watch him walk around the front of the car. Then, a gunshot. It sound rang in my ear. The thump in my chest felt like it would burst through my ribs. I collapsed onto the center console and made eye contact with O'Ryan. I saw the glimmer of a tear catch the full moon's light. He mouthed "I'm sorry" before falling to the ground out of sight.

"He's back," I squeaked only loud enough for me to hear.

I covered my mouth to hold back a whimper and fell onto the floor facing Bryan.

"Stay down," Bryan said. He slowly got up holding his ribs with one hand, using the other hand for support. I moved to the left as he came closer. He leaned over the center console and locked the passenger door. He grunted and turned to the driver's door twisted in ways he shouldn't, and reached for the lock. I heard the quiet thump of the lock go down. Bryan rested on the center console holding his ribs.

"Bryan?"

I stepped over Justin's legs while I was bent over and moved to behind the driver's seat. I looked through the crack in between the driver's door and the shoulder of the seat. Crazy man came into view and I knew he could have a clear shot at Bryan if I didn't move him.

"Bryan," I said in a high whisper as I walked to him in a crouch. I put my hands on his thighs. "Come on."

I got up and bent myself over, making myself a clear target. I grabbed Bryan's shoulders, and with my legs and arms I pulled him up. He yelled in pain and grabbed my shoulder with one hand, his ribs with the other.

"I know," I said. "I'm sorry."

I had tears in my eyes from fear and knowing that I could feel their pain. Not only do I have to keep them alive, but now I have to defend them.

Chapter 10

I got Bryan on the floor next to his brother, and sat down in fetal position next to him. As I heard footsteps get closer I looked down at Bryan without any idea of what to do.

Bryan slowly sat up and edged his way toward the door. I quickly grabbed his shoulder. "What are you doing?"

"Protecting you," he said not much higher than a whisper.

"That's not your job," I said as I slowly turned his shoulder until he was facing me.

"Your protector is out of commission for right now. I'm the next one in line."

I looked up to the human figure that was now standing outside the passenger door. He lifted the butt end of the gun and slammed it into the window. Bryan covered me, forgetting about the pain in his ribs. I looked up from Bryan's shoulder when I didn't feel any glass. The window spider webbed, but didn't break.

"Stay here. Protect Justin," Bryan said squeezing me tight. I saw Crazy man lift the gun again and hit the window. Little tiny glass pieces sprayed the interior of the car, and Justin. Bryan covered me with his body until the last glass diamond fell then lightly pushed me back towards Justin.

Bryan looked to Crazy man who was trying to clear the glass away from the window's edge. He grabbed the end of the gun and tried to pull it from Crazy's hands, but was instead pulled out of the window, across the new sharp glass and out of my sight. I used every ounce of will power I had to not go after him. *I'm not going to just sit here.* I looked down at Justin and saw little cut marks from the broken glass pieces. I picked the small pieces off that were still on his face, and put my hand to his cheek. I slowly lowered myself and gently kissed him on the lips. I lifted myself back up to a sitting position and held his hand hoping it wouldn't be the last time feeling his skin.

"Thank you for protecting me, but now, it's my turn."

As I turned to leave I felt his hand take hold of mine. "I can't let you do that."

"Let go!" I said sternly through gritted teeth. "Bryan is out there. It's my turn to protect you and him."

"I promised your brother Heather. What would he do if something happened to you," he shot back with pauses to grunt and whimper.

"Andrew isn't here," I yelled.

I yanked my arm out of Justin's grip and toward the danger I thought I would never have to face.

I hesitated at the door, but could hear Bryan fighting. I could hear fist hitting bone, and cries for help. I felt Justin's hand on my shoulder and bursted through the door. I jumped from the car and saw Bryan on the bottom. I threw myself onto the man's back, and wrapped my arm around his neck.

Andrew and I were always play fighting. He taught me wrestling holds and all the ways to defend myself if it ever came down to it.

I quickly put a sleeper hold under Crazy's chin and squeezed for as long as my muscles would allow. Bryan got out from under us and looked toward the other cars.

"Heather," I faintly heard Bryan say. My arms were burning and it seemed like there was no use in continuing. Crazy was pretty much clawing at my arms. I could feel my blood seeping through the scratches he had opened, but I wouldn't give up even though the hold wasn't doing anything.

I guess Bryan could tell the hold wasn't working. Even though he was cut up, and bloodied he jumped back in to help me. He started to hit Crazy repeatedly while I still had him in the hold.

"Bryan," I heard Justin's voice say. I looked to Bryan, but there was no response.

"Bryan," I said letting go of the hold. I fell to the ground and crawled backwards. I slowly got up, "Bryan, don't kill him."

I looked to Justin.

"Bryan," Justin yelled.

He stopped, "What!"

"Stop," Justin said in normal tone, holding his broken rib.

Bryan finally looked at Crazy. He was not unconscious, but certainly was beat up. Bryan looked at his blood covered knuckles, then to me.

"I'm, uh."

I slowly approached Bryan lifting my hand to place on his neck. "It's done."

Bryan brought me in for a hug, and that's when I noticed a crowd had formed around us. As I hugged Bryan I could still feel motion from Crazy. The crowd started to disperse and I could hear footsteps coming from the direction of the accident.

"It's about time they showed up," I said in a whisper with a hint of sarcasm.

"I know, took them long enough."

Bryan released me, but kept his hands on my hips, mine on his shoulders.

Crazy spit blood on the pavement to get my attention.

"You were asking for it," I said.

"Why did you stop," Crazy said egging Bryan on. "We were just getting started."

"I had my share of humiliating someone tonight. I'm good for a while." A smile had spread across Crazy's face.

Bryan put his hand on my lower back and pushed me toward the car. About halfway to the car I heard the click of a gun being cocked and looked to my right. I saw his rifle sitting on the pavement.

"Put the gun down," a man yelled.

By the time I turned my head I felt the wind being knocked out of me.

Chapter 11

Justin

She fell in slow motion, and the few feet in between her and I felt like miles. I felt her dead weight as she landed in my arms.

"Justin," she cried softly.

"Don't talk," I said calmly turning her face towards me. "You're okay, we just have to get you to a hospital."

While her eyes tried to stay open I looked at the gunshot wound. Her long sleeve shirt was stained red.

The police showed up seconds after the incident and took Crazy away, hopefully for good this time.

"Put pressure on the wound," a bystander said. I looked up with tear filled eyes as a young lady calmly, but quickly came over. "Lay her down. Do you have something to wrap around her waist. Once we stop the bleeding the wrap should last until you get to the closest hospital. It's only twenty minutes from here."

Bryan has gotten up and to my surprise he handed the young lady a first aid kit. He came to kneel next to me, as we watched this young stranger help us.

"Where did you find this?" I asked putting my one free hand on Heather's gunshot hole.

"I packed it for some strange reason."

Tears blurred my vision and all these thoughts rushed through my head. *How will I live like this? He trusted me and now she's* . . I pushed the thought away knowing it won't come true.

We went through all the gauze in the kit and was able to slow the bleeding

I helped lift Heather so she could to wrap the bandage tightly, then she tied it off right over the gunshot. I felt Bryan put his hand on my shoulder so his forearm was resting parallel my back. I heard more footsteps and looked to the EMS coming. I still held Heather in the same spot as when I caught her. I couldn't look away.

"We had called these guys about an hour ago for you," Bryan said. "They are here under different circumstances." He lifted my chin until my eyes met with his. "She will be okay."

Bryan and I got up slowly with pain in our ribs after give EMS took Heather. When she was in the safe hands of EMS and out of my sight did I notice the young lady standing in front of me.

"Are you kids okay?" she asked.

"Banged up," I said. "But were fine."

"May I look?" she asked gently touching my hand that was on my ribs. Her hands were warm and seemed to wash away the chill of the night that just happened. She took my hand away, lifted my shirt and gently placed her hand on the indent where my rib used to be. "It'll need surgery to avoid any further damage to the lung."

"How do you know?" I asked.

"I've been doing these kinds of assessments for eleven years." I looked to Bryan not realizing how much older she is than I am. "It becomes easy once you know what to look for."

"Thank you, for everything."

"May I help you to an ambulance?" she asked me then looked to Bryan.

"Yes please."

As we walked all I could think of was Heather and how I wasn't with her. *What would Andrew do if she doesn't make it? What would I do?*

I hung my head low as I walked. The lady was holding my hand, leading Bryan and I to an ambulance.

"Justin," Bryan said.

"What?" I snapped, and felt a sharp pain against my side.

"I'm sorry for anything I might have done last night."

"Why are you sorry?" I asked looking back to him.

"I don't know."

"Come here," I said waving him up next to me. "It's my fault if anyone's."

"You did what you had to do," he said.

"I hope so."

We got to a lone ambulance on the shoulder of the road. The crash sight was clear of smashed cars and broken bodies. Only the glass debris remains. The lady turned to leave after looking at Bryan, "I never got your name?"

"Brea," she said walking back to where the traffic was waiting eagerly to get moving.

"What about my car?" I asked.

"We have a police officer driving it to the hospital we are taking you," the EMS guy said.

"What hospital?" Brea asked.

"Did someone get O'Ryan?" I asked.

"Yes he was killed on sight."

"Heathworks Hospital, in Allentown. It's the closest," the EMS guy said in a rush.

"When was this?" I asked.

"Justin, you were unconscious most of the night," Bryan said.

The EMS guy and lady got the bed out from the back of the truck then asked me to lay down. I had a pain shoot through my side when I bent to sit down, but it subsided when I lay down. I could only breathe shallow, and the pain was worse now than before.

"What's her name?" Brea asked.

"Heather," I teared. "Heather Mackentire."

Brea put her hand on mine. "I'll meet you there."

She left without me saying thank you. I looked back to Bryan.

"Is that why everything is a blur? I don't remember much," I tried to say.

"Not even the fight?"

"What fight?" I grunted.

"The fight when you broke your rib?"

"I don't remember."

They got me up into the truck and Bryan got in before they closed the doors.

Chapter 12

EMS rolled me through the entrance of the hospital. There was a small bump in between the concrete of the sidewalk and the tile of the hospital that vibrated up the bed's wheels into my ribs. They rolled me pass the front desk while Bryan followed. The EMS guy promised Bryan and I could share a room. I finally relaxed my head against the pillow when we passed under a sign that said surgery. *Heather could be here. She could be in surgery right now.*

"Bryan," I said holding my hand out. He came into view and walked backwards to look at me. "Look for Heather please."

"They want us to stay together," he said.

"When we get to our room, please go find her," I pleaded.

"If they let me. I will." He put his hand on mine.

"Your surgery is scheduled for ten o'clock this morning. If we can get you in earlier, we will," the nurse said. I hadn't realized the nurse's had taken over for the EMS guys. *Wow, I am so out of it.*

"Rest now," the nurse said. "We will wake you before we move you."

"Thank you," I said low.

The room was quiet after the nurse got me situated and left. I looked at Bryan and even though there was really nothing to say, I, for once, enjoyed his company.

"You did good tonight Bryan."

"My brother taught me well," he said.

I chuckled and felt a pain surge through me. I grabbed my ribs and moved into a comfortable position.

"Do you need any stitches?" I asked after I noticed the gash on his forehead.

"I hope not. I don't like needles."

The next nurse that came into my room brought me breakfast.

"Do you know anything about Heather Mackentire?" I asked.

"She's still in surgery."

"How long has it been?"

"Two hours. Who are you in relation?" the nurse asked nicely.

"Her guardian, brother, friend. Whatever you would like to put me down as. Do you know when she will be done?"

With a smile, "I don't know sir. If I hear anything I will be sure to let you know."

"If I'm not around, Bryan here is my brother. Also her guardian."

"I'll be sure to let you know," she said quietly then left.

"I'm nervous," I said.

"You'll be fine," Bryan said getting up from the chair to stand by my bed.

"Not about my surgery, about hers. I know we stopped the bleeding, but that was after she lost so much. I can't stand to lose her."

Heather of course is pretty much my younger sister. She has become my soft spot ever since Andrew gave me the responsibility. I have failed him.

"You won't lose her. You know how strong she is," Bryan said trying to reassure me.

"Yes, but sometimes being strong isn't enough."

I starred at the white ceiling through my tears until sleep took me.

• • •

I could see Heather lying on the surgery table with her eyes closed and shirt open. There was no blood because her wound seemed to be wrapped. I took a step forward and put my forehead against the window and everything changed.

There were doctors calmly working on her wound trying to retrieve the bullet that never exited her body. There was a nurse at her head holding a mask on her nose and mouth. That must me the anesthesia.

"Her pulse is dropping," a woman said right before the long beep of no heartbeat.

"Heather," I yelled. If I had the strength to bust through the window I would have, but everything felt numb.

● ● ●

"Heather," I said and woke with a jump.

"Justin," Bryan said. "It was a dream dude. It's okay."

I looked at Bryan who was now sitting in a chair at my side. I calmed my breathing and tried to push the pain out when a nurse came in.

"Heather is out of surgery. She's in recovery."

"Oh, thank god," I said squeezing Bryan's hand.

"I told you."

"It's time for you to get fixed up," the lady nurse said as two guy nurses came in. Bryan got up and pushed the chair back against the wall.

"I'll see you soon," Bryan said as they pushed me toward surgery

Chapter 13

Heather

The last thing I could remember was Bryan wrapping his arms around me in a hug after Crazy man got beat up.

I was starring at a white ceiling feeling drowsy and a little loopy. I moved my head to look at the door that seemed to be floating. I turned my body to face the door when I felt a pain down my entire right side. I screamed and instantly heard footsteps rush in through the black dots in my vision.

"Heather, it's okay dear. You just got out of surgery. It'll take some time to heal."

"What am I doing here?" I asked scared and confused.

"Do you remember the traffic on Highway 78?" the nurse asked me.

"Yes, I just don't know how I ended up here. Where is Justin? And Bryan," I panicked.

I wanted to get out of bed to find them, but I could barely sit up, let alone walk the halls.

"Justin and Bryan know you're here. Justin is going in for surgery for his broken rib," she explained. "Bryan is getting his rib patched up. I'll try to find them for you. Let's lay you on your back. You need to rest my dear."

"Thank you," I said with tired eyes.

• • •

"Heather?" I heard in a daze. "Heather."

I opened my eyes and tried to see who it was through my blurry, foggy vision.

"Heather, oh my god. I found you."

"Bryan," I said in a high whisper.

"Don't try to talk. It'll be okay now."

I felt his hand grab mine, and another hand on my cheek.

"You look great," he said.

I chuckled. "That's and understatement," I said moving to sit up a little. "How's Justin." I was able to focus my eyes looking at the TV and brought my eyes down to see Bryan. "Oh my goodness. Bryan?"

"I'm fine. The nurse told me it doesn't need stitches."

"When will I see Justin?" I asked trying to keep my eyes open.

"A few days when you're both a little stronger to sit up," he smiled.

"Have we called Cathy yet?" I asked, my voice still groggy from no use.

"No," he replied.

"Maybe we should. We are like twenty minutes from her house."

I wanted to sit up even though I couldn't keep my eyes open. I really didn't want to lie down anymore, but my wound wouldn't let me.

"Heather, stop being so stubborn. You can't sit up. Stop trying," Bryan said placing his hands on my shoulders.

"Fine," I pouted and lay back down. "I hate being on my back."

"Deal with it." He smiled.

Bryan kept me company all day. He had gone over to the corner of the room multiple times. It took me hours to realize our luggage was what he kept going over to.

"Cards?" he suggested.

"Sure. Can't say I'll be able to stay awake through the whole thing. "Go fish?" I said a little higher than a whisper.

"We'll try. Sure, sounds good.

● ● ●

"Room 127C," I heard coming out of sleep. I opened my eyes and could feel cards still in my hand. I heard a bed being placed on the other side of the curtain. "Bryan."

He was in the chair asleep, leaning his head on the bed next to my hand. "Bryan?"

"Uhh."

"Can you open the curtain? It might be Justin."

"Heather," he said putting both elbows on the bed. "What are the odds of *them* putting *him* in the same room as *us*."

"I don't care about the odds. Open the curtain," I yelled.

A pain shot through my entire right side. It felt as if someone stabbed me and is ripping a hole in my skin. Almost instantly the room around me started to fade out. I could hear my machine's quick beeping with the sound of my heartbeat. I saw Bryan come into view one last time before my vision went black. I could hear Justin yelling and Bryan's voice trying to console him.

"Help her!" he yelled.

He's awake.

Chapter 14

I could feel a soft touch running up and down my arm. I slowly moved my fingers around the hand that had stopped on top of mine. I slowly turned my head and saw the brightness of the ceiling's lights though my eyelids. I swallowed what salvia I could muster to relieve my cottonmouth.

"Open your eyes Heather."

It took every ounce of strength I had to open them. My vision was still foggy with sleep, and I was so beyond out of it.

"Justin."

"I'm here."

I felt his hand grab mine and looked down at my hand. He was standing next to my bed with regular clothes on.

"Where am I?"

"Hospital," I heard Cathy say.

"There's a few people here to see you," Bryan said.

"Cathy!" I tried to yell through dry lips, but my voice came out hoarse and ragged. "I'm thirsty."

"Well, your only source of water has been through your arm. I'd be thirsty too," Justin smiled.

He held a small cup of apple juice and put the straw to my mouth.

"That tastes amazing." I looked to Cathy. "You couldn't have waited until I got out. I look like crap," I said low with my eyes still closed.

"You look pretty good considering you got shot and just came out of a coma."

"How long?' I asked.

No one answered.

"I'm sorry." I closed my eyes and lifted my free hand to my head. I felt too weak to cry, but my body did anyway.

"Heather." It was Justin. My cheeks were soaked with salty tears. "Everything is okay. We are alive," he assure me.

"No reason to be sorry," Cathy said softly.

I looked down to see her at the foot of my bed.

"Who's that?' I asked looking at the door.

Justin turned around to the door. "Brea."

"It looks like she is doing very well," she said still standing at the door.

Justin invited her in. "Heather, this is Brea. She helped us to stop the bleeding after. . ."

"Uh-huh." I looked at Brea and held up my hand. "Thank you."

"The nurse said she'll be back around three," Bryan told us.

"What day is it?"

"Thursday." Justin said.

How you feeling?" Cathy asked.

"Tired."

"Maybe you should get some rest," she suggested.

"Can she say hi to me first?" I know that voice. I slowly turned my achy head to the door. "Heather."

His voice echoed through my room even though he wasn't yelling. I opened my eyes and tried to focus through sleep. I was finally able to see who it was. He came over to me in his uniform. It was my brother.

"Andrew?" I asked low.

"Who else would it be?"

I gave a short laugh then held my side.

"We got stuck in a predicament."

"Yeah," he smiled taking hold of my hand. I knew for sure I wasn't dreaming. He was really here. "Looks like it. How you feeling?"

"Tired. How, how did you get here? I was only asleep for a few hours."

Andrew looked back at Bryan. "No, you weren't. Before your 'sleep', you kind of yelled at me to open the curtain. When you yelled the stitches in your side opened back up and you lost a fair amount of blood. You slipped into a coma. You've been asleep for two weeks."

I looked back to Andrew. He was really here. I could feel his hand on top of mine. His hand was warm when he touched my cheek. I lifted my hand and put it on top of his.

"Andrew," I said threw a few fallen tears. "You're really here."

"I'm really here," he said.

"I've missed you. How long have you been waiting?" I asked getting emotional.

"It's okay," Andrew said squeezing my hand. "You're awake now, that's all that matters."

There was silence, then Andrew spoke again. "Justin was able to stabilize your blood loss."

"What?" I asked confused. I looked to Justin who was lifting rolling up his sleeve. In the crook of his elbow was a white square held on with white tape.

"We have the same blood type." He smiled.

Tears blurred my vision and laughter quietly filled the room.

The laughter subsided and was followed by the shuffling of feet heading towards the door. I didn't want anyone to leave, but I was hoping Andrew and I would get this time.

"You're like a wounded solider," he said.

"Yeah, but I didn't sacrifice my life for my country. You fight to survive everyday."

"Yes, but you're a hero to Justin, and Bryan. You saved them."

"Are you coming home with me?"

"Yeah, I'm home for about three weeks before my next deployment."

"Does that mean I won't see Justin and Bryan for three weeks?"

"Heather, they pretty much live with us. Why don't you have them move in," he joked.

"Sarcasm?"

"No, for real," his smile was soft, and contagious, just like I remembered.

Andrew put his hand on my head and kissed me gently on the forehead. "You can rest easy. None of us are going anywhere."

● ● ●

My three days went by faster that I expected. Andrew had slept with me in the bed for both nights. Bryan usually slept in the chair under the window. Cathy wound up sleeping on the floor, and Justin didn't look like he slept at all

Andrew helped me out to the car and I thanked the nurses at the front desk on the way by.

"Did Brea leave?"

"Yeah, yesterday, but she gave me her number to keep her updated on how you're doing."

Justin opened the door to his SUV while Cathy and Bryan got our bags into the back.

"Is that the only reason she gave you her number?" I asked as if it was so obvious.

"Heather, she's ten years older, besides, I have my girl right here."

I smiled and couldn't help the butterflies that fluttered in my tummy when he said that.

"Are we going home or to Cathy's?" I asked looking to Justin while Andrew helped me into the car.

"We didn't come all this way just to go back home. We could all use a few hours sleep at Cathy's place. Besides, I really don't want to get stuck in rush hour traffic."

www.ingramcontent.com/pod-product-compliance
Lightning Source LLC
Chambersburg PA
CBHW020646130626
46552CB00003B/1415